elongs to

SA

For Nick Dewar,
whose doodles were always better than mine

First published in Great Britain in 2011 by

Gullane Children's Books

185 Fleet Street, London, EC4A 2HS
www.gullanebooks.com

This paperback edition first published in 2012

10   9   8   7   6   5   4   3   2   1

Text and illustrations © Ross Collins 2011

The right of Ross Collins to be identified as the author and illustrator of this work has
been asserted by him in accordance with the Copyright, Designs and Patents Act, 1988.
A CIP record for this title is available from the British Library.

ISBN: 978-1-86233-847-0

Printed and bound in China

Doodleday is a (brilliant) work of fiction with no link to National Doodle Day, a (worthy and
brilliant) fund-raising event held annually in support of the charities Epilepsy Action and the
Neurofibromatosis Association, which provide support and advice for children and adults affected
by epilepsy and neurofibromatosis.

Epilepsy Action (234343) and The Neurofibromatosis Association (1078790) are both registered charities in England

Mo

9

8

6 7

6

Doodleday

15

14

13

by Ross Collins

22

20 21

GULLANE
CHILDREN'S BOOKS

29

"I'm going to the shops now," said Harvey's mum.
"Don't bother your dad — he's tied up with work."
"Fine," said Harvey. "I'll just do some drawing."

"DRAWI

...NG?"

shrieked Mum, snatching the pencil from Harvey's hand.

**"DRAWING...
on Doodleday?
Are you mad?"**

"What's **Doodleday?**" asked Harvey.

**"NOBODY
draws on
Doodleday**
and that's that!"

"Why does..." Harvey began, but Mum was already gone.

As soon as Mum was out of sight, Harvey took
out the pencils he kept in his secret shoebox.
"Doodleday indeed," thought Harvey.
He'd never heard such rubbish.
One small drawing couldn't hurt a fly.

"That's it," thought Harvey.

"I'll draw a fly."

It was an excellent fly.

Fat...

and hairy

and...

BUZZZZZZZZZ

What was that noise in the kitchen?

"**My fly!**" gasped Harvey.
Harvey's fly was fat, hairy and **ENORMOUS**,
and it was **destroying the kitchen**.
Harvey was worried –
no flypaper would work on this monster.
"What gets rid of flies?" he thought. "Spiders! That's it!
Spiders eat flies for breakfast!"

Harvey ran back to the lounge and quickly
drew a big, hairy spider.

But **Harvey's spider**
didn't care for flies.
It was far more interested
in his dad.

Harvey wondered if
a drawing could eat you.
He wasn't going to wait to find out…

"What eats spiders? Birds! That's it! Birds love eating spiders!"
Harvey drew a great big bird, with talons and a big, bug-munching beak.

As soon as Harvey finished drawing, he heard a terrifying

SQUAWK!

from outside.

There above the house was **Harvey's bird.**

And there was Mr Bagshaw's fence,

being turned into a nest.

Mr Bagshaw wasn't happy at all…

… and neither were the other neighbours.

"Are these your drawings, Harvey?"

"Don't you know it's
Doodleday?"

"You sort this out RIGHT NOW, young man!"

"**Huge,**" thought Harvey.
"Only something **huge**
could reach up there."

Harvey grabbed his pad and drew
the biggest creature in the world…

The Giant Squid decided to
DESTROY the STREET.

"Mum!" cried Harvey…

"**What were you thinking, Harvey?**" yelled Mum.
"It's Doodleday!"

"**I didn't mean to!**" cried Harvey.
Mum grabbed the pad and started to scribble furiously.

Harvey couldn't see what she was drawing.

What could **swat** a giant fly?

Eat a gigantic spider?

Bring down a monstrous bird?

Be **more ferocious** than a Giant Squid?

Mum drew...

Mum! Doodle Mum walked calmly up the street, gave a little cough and bellowed...

Mum held open
the pad.

In buzzed the **fly**.

In crawled the **spider**.

In flew the **bird**.

In squeezed the **squid**.

"Thank you kindly," said Mum.
"My pleasure," said Doodle Mum.
She shook Mum's hand politely and stepped inside.

With a **SNAP**, the pad was shut.

Harvey's mum scratched her head and sighed.
"Now help me get your father
down from that lamppost."

"Is Doodleday every year...?"

asked Harvey.

Other books for you to enjoy . . .

Cloth From the Clouds
Michael Catchpool • illustrated by Alison Jay

On top of a hill, a boy spins cloth from the clouds, just enough for a
warm scarf. But when the King sees the wonderful cloth, he demands
cloaks and gowns galore. "It would not be wise," the boy protests.
"Your majesty does not need them!" But spin he must – and soon
the world around him begins to change . . .

Charles Fuge's Astonishing Animal ABC

An Arty Aardvark, a Dancing Dodo, an Outraged Owl and a Sleepy Sloth
are just some of the astonishing creatures in this highly original animal
alphabet. Marvel at their extraordinary antics – and try to guess
which fantastic creature is zig-zag-zooming its way to Z . . .!

That Yucky Love Thing
Michael Catchpool • illustrated by Victoria Ball

Everywhere Sam looks, people are hugging and kissing – it's disgusting!
Even in the middle of the jungle and the depths of the ocean there's no
escape. So how will Sam feel when he slips and falls . . . and finds a little
girl reaching out her hand to him?!

For more fantastic books for children, visit
www.gullanebooks.com.